This book belongs to

....

Written by Rosie Greening.
Illustrated by Edward Miller.

LITTLE RED GINGERBREAD

Rosie Greening • Edward Miller

make
believe
ideas

In a fairy-tale forest
lived young Baker **FRED**,
who was **famous** for making
the best **gingerbread**.

FLOUR

JANUARY

1	2	3	4	5	6	7
8	9	10	11	12	13	14
15	16	17	18	19	20	21
22	23	24	25	26	27	28
29	30	31			GRAN'S BIRTHDAY	

One day, FRED cried out,

"I NEED GiFTS FOR GRAN!"

So he started to make her a gingerbread man.

He baked it

and iced it,

but then gave a cry

as the SNACK made a cape
from some red cloth nearby.

Then all of a sudden, the treat yelled, "**SURPRISE!**

I'm Little Red Gingerbread, and I'm *ALIVE!*"

The small, **sneaky** snack
started **R U N N I N G** away,
so Fred **chased** him, shouting:
"Get back on your tray!"

But the treat was too fast,
and he called back with **GLEE**:

"I'm Little Red
Gingerbread —
**YOU CAN'T
CATCH ME!**"

He **whizzed** past a bear
who was **hunting** for HONEY.

"**STOP!**"
the bear **shouted.**
"Your icing looks
YUMMY."

But Little Red sang,
as he CLIMBED up a tree:
"I'm Little Red Gingerbread –
YOU CAN'T CATCH ME!"

He **perched** on
a tree branch,
ENJOYING
the breeze...

...when something
ENORMOUS
SWOOPED
out of the trees.

It was Owl,
on the hunt
for a SNACK
she could eat.

"STOP!" ordered Owl. "What a hootiful treat."

But Little Red JUMPED
from the branch, crying:
"WHEEEEE!

I'm Little Red Gingerbread –
YOU CAN'T CATCH ME!"

He RAN through the forest,
not looking ahead.

Then —

CRASH!

He bumped into SQUIRREL instead.

Squirrel was searching for ACORNS to crunch.
"You look like a nut," he said. "Perfect for lunch!"

Through a gate,
up a path,
to a doorway he ran,
STRAIGHT into
the cottage of
Baker Fred's gran!

He **CHARGED** through the house and found Gran in her bed.

"WHAT BIG EARS YOU HAVE!" cried the RUDE gingerbread.

But Gran had a plan,
so she shouted,

"PiG GEARS?

I'm too DEAF to hear you –
come closer, my dear!"

He hopped,
SKIPPED, and jumped
on the bed next to Gran.
"WHAT BiG TEETH
YOU HAVE!"
cried the
gingerbread man.

"WiG THiEF?"

roared Gran,

with a big, SNEAKY grin.

"I really can't HEAR you –
come up to my chin."

So Little Red Gingerbread
LEAPED to the place,
as Gran hid the sniggers
and SMILE on her face.

Then, quick as a F☺X,
before he could escape,
Gran **SWALLOWED**
the GINGERBREAD
AND his red cape!

That night in the **bakery**,
FRED got a note:

Fred **smiled** as he worked on his **NEXT** baking plan:
three little gingerbread pigs for his **gran**!